"Hey, Sadie! Did you hear about Little Amy Scott?
About how she got a goldfish for her birthday, and then said out loud . . .

"And how she walked all the way out of town, past the empty school bus,
 and down to the dock where Jacob Finney's been asleep for as long as I can remember?"

"Imagine that poor fish all alone, floating away, and away, and away. He must feel like . . .

To Lily Anna —P. S.

To Phil —M. C.

Text copyright © 2017 by Philip C. Stead
Illustrations copyright © 2017 by Matthew Cordell
A Neal Porter Book
Published by Roaring Brook Press
Roaring Brook Press is a division of Holtzbrinck Publishing Holdings Limited Partnership
175 Fifth Avenue, New York, New York 10010
The artwork for this book was created using pen and ink with watercolor.
mackids.com

Cataloging-in-Publication Data is on file at the Library of Congress

ISBN: 978-1-62672-282-8

Our books may be purchased in bulk for promotional, educational, or business use. Please
contact your local bookseller or the Macmillan Corporate and Premium Sales Department
at (800) 221-7945 ext. 5442 or by e-mail at MacmillanSpecialMarkets@macmillan.com.

First edition 2017
Book design by Philip C. Stead and Matthew Cordell
Printed in China by RR Donnelley Asia printing Solutions Ltd.,Dongguan City,Guangdong Province

1 3 5 7 9 10 8 6 4 2

The Only Fish in the sea

written by
Philip C. Stead

illustrated by
Matthew Cordell

click!

A Neal Porter Book   Roaring Brook Press   New York

"What do you think about that, Sadie? . . . Sadie?"

"That's terrible, Sherman."

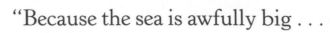

"Because the sea is awfully big . . .

. . . and there are a lot of dangers to face."

"The important thing, Sherman, is that Ellsworth stays hopeful and brave,
knowing that we're on our way."

"Hey, Sadie, wait! Who's Ellsworth?"

"Sherman, you have to keep up. Every fish deserves a proper name."

"Now, we'll need to borrow a boat . . .

click!

a net, and two long fishing poles . . .

twenty-one pink balloons . . .

a bucket of paint . . .

and appropriate headwear in case of weather—good or bad.

Then, with any luck, Sherman . . .

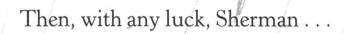

we'll catch a fish in time for dinner."

"In the meantime, we'll have tea. Patience, Sherman, is the most important part of fishing."

"Sadie?"

"Yes, Sherman?"

"Are we eating Ellsworth for dinner tonight?"

"Sherman, no!"

"We'll give him a home and find him a nice place to sit and be a fish—

LIBRARY

BAIT AND TACKLE, ETC.

SCHOOL

SLH

SPLOOSH!

somewhere with a view
of the entire neighborhood."

"When he is hungry we will feed him."

"And when he is lonely
we will keep him company."

"Ellsworth will feel lucky to have so many friends."

"Sadie?"

"Yes, Sherman?"

"What about Little Amy Scott?"

"Sherman, she'll spend her birthday alone."

SQUEEZE

"And that's all right."